Help with reading aloud

- If you have time, try reading the book by yourself first. Practise reading it out loud.
- You may not know all the words, but don't worry. If you are not sure how to say a word, split it up into parts and sound it out, e.g. comfortable would be com-for-ta-ble.
- If you are not sure what a word means, look at the pictures to see if there are any clues that may help.
- Some of the names are made up for the Amazing Travelling Space Circus. Look at the pages at the front of the book which show all the characters.

Next step

If you would like to find more help with reading, there are BBC RaW book groups all round the country. Call 0800 0150 950 to find your nearest RaW centre and to get some free advice on what to do next. Or visit our website (bbc.co.uk/raw) and enter your postcode to find your nearest RaW centre.

Published by the BBC
201 Wood Lane
London W12 7TS

© BBC 2007
All rights reserved.
Reproduction in whole or in part prohibited without permission.

ISBN 978-1-86000-239-7

Written by Heather Morris

Illustrated by Peter Lawson

Characters created by Firedog Design

Designed by Starfish Design, Editorial and Project Management Ltd

Printed in Great Britain by ESP Colour Ltd

Printed on paper manufactured from sustainable forests

In this book you will meet ...

Guv
the Ringmaster
Always busy running the circus – he's loved by everyone. He's quite old and needs his aerial soapbox to get around.

Mrs. Spectacles
The Ringmaster's wife, she runs the circus. She's a clever old woman who plans everything and looks after everyone.

Hover Bugs
They are very clever machines that can suck up rubbish and turn it into flowers on planet Polyma.

Bamrod
the Blender
Bamrod is a scientist and a maker of potions that don't often work. But once or twice he gets it right!

Gobi
the Circus Roustabout
He's the circus handyman. Gobi's only happy when inventing, fixing or playing with machines. He sulks if people don't pay attention to him.

Baked Bean
A shy green dragon who has just learnt to fly and breathe fire like other dragons. But he can't always control it.

Tiny
the Strongoid
A tiny girl who loves to play. She's pretty but so strong she often breaks things. She's very helpful.

Mr. Scatterbrain
the Clown
He loves to entertain people and make them laugh. He usually rides a jet-powered unicorn.

Max
Max is Lara's elder brother. He is quite creative and has a good sense of humour. He is a good friend of the circus.

Lara
Lara is Max's younger sister. She really likes Max and feels safe with him. She also loves the circus.

Monstro
the Master of Disguise
He has many talents and can grow new arms when things get busy

Dom and Dee
They are with Green Force TV and come to help the circus clean up the mess, but they are too busy filming to do much work.

The circus has been on planet Polyma for two weeks and now it is all packed up and ready to leave. But the site is a mess. There is rubbish everywhere, the grass is trampled flat and plants are damaged. A tree has even been pushed over. There is a burnt patch on the ground and some drooping flowers

where Baked Bean has been practising breathing fire. Things on planet Polyma melt rather easily.

Guv and Mrs. Spectacles, who run the circus, are not happy.

Mrs. Spectacles orders a clean-up. It's very quick and easy on planet Polyma. She whistles loudly and a team of Hover Bugs appears. They whizz round the site and suck up all the rubbish.

They are very clever as they can grind up the rubbish and mix it all together. Then they turn this into brand new flowers. Soon the grass is clean.

Now it's Bamrod's turn. He is a scientist and maker of potions. Not all of them work but he has made a special potion that restores the grass and plants on planet Polyma. One blast of his spray and the grass stands up again and the flowers get back their colours.

Mrs. Spectacles looks around. The site is starting to look better. But there is still the fallen tree. She thinks for a moment and then calls to Tiny. Tiny is the circus strong girl. She is so strong that she often breaks things by accident but she is also very helpful.

'Do you think you could put the tree back?' Mrs. Spectacles asks her. Tiny just looks at it and says, 'No problem.' She simply picks it up and pops it back in the hole. The tree clicks into place and looks as good as new.

The last problem is the burnt patch of ground where Baked Bean has been practising breathing fire. He is very excited that he can do this, but he can't always control it. Gobi is the circus handyman and he can mend most things. He paints over the melted patch and it looks fine again.

Mrs. Spectacles has one last look around. Planet Polyma's magic plastic looks just as good as it did before the circus arrived.

'I love planet Polyma,' she says happily, 'it's so quick and easy to clean.' They all climb into the spacecraft and the space circus blasts off. Their next stop is planet Earth.

Would you like to live on planet Polyma?

After a long trip, the space circus touches down on planet Earth. They are very excited to be visiting because two good friends of the circus, Max and Lara, live there.

They are all very pleased to see each other again. Since they last met, the circus has several new acts and Max and Lara are looking forward to

watching the show. Best of all their favourite dragon, Baked Bean, has learned to fly and to breathe fire.

News of the circus spreads quickly and it is so successful that they stay for a month. Finally it is time to leave and the circus packs up again. Only this time, there is a big problem....

This time when they look around the site, it is even worse than on planet Polyma. Visitors have left rubbish all over the place, even in the pond. The grass is brown and muddy, the plants are bent and broken. A young tree has been snapped and the bird who had started to build her nest there is flying round anxiously.

Lara and Max are shocked. 'What a mess,' says Max. 'What can we do?' asks Lara.

'Don't worry', says Mrs. Spectacles. 'I am sure we can clean it up in no time.'

Do you think the clean-up will work?

But it's not as simple as on planet Polyma. There are no Hover Bugs here so Monstro grows some extra arms and tries to collect the rubbish. But his arms get in a tangle and the rubbish is even more mixed-up.

Bamrod tries his potion on the flat grass. But instead of growing up straight, it starts to turn brown. 'Stop, stop!' Lara cries, 'You're making it worse.'

Tiny is trying to help by holding up the broken tree, but as soon as she lets go it

just flops over again. She is puzzled, 'I can't mend this.' The poor bird who was building her nest in the tree flies round cheeping loudly.

By now everyone in the circus is worried. They are all hot and tired but nothing they do seems to help. Gobi doesn't even dare to try his special paint. Baked Bean is running round in circles because he doesn't know what to do.

Things are different on planet Earth.

What do you think they should do?

17

Lara calls Guv and Mrs. Spectacles inside the spacecraft. She and Max could see the problems and have been searching the space screen for advice.

Guv and Mrs. Spectacles join them in front of the screen. 'We don't know what's gone wrong. We managed to fix everything really quickly on planet Polyma but it's not working here,' Mrs. Spectacles says.

'How can we clear up this mess?' Guv asks.

'We don't know,' says Max, 'but we've found some people who might help. We'll call in the Green Force team.'

Guv and Mrs. Spectacles look at each other, 'Who are they?'

Who do you think Green Force are?

The Green Force team arrives really quickly. 'Hi, I'm Dom and this is Dee,' says the man. 'We're the Green Force team – we do makeovers,' Dee adds. Before Mrs. Spectacles can reply, they rush off to take a quick look round the site.

'What a mess! This will make great TV,' says Dom. 'You have two days to sort this out before the show.'

'Will you help us?' asks Mrs Spectacles.

'Oh no, we'll be too busy filming,' Dee replies, 'We'll just tell you what to do.'

The circus crew are not too happy but they are too scared to say anything.

'OK, you must start with the rubbish,' Dee says. 'You need to sort it out as you collect it. Hey, you with the six arms, you should be good at this.'

Monstro starts to explain how he got all tangled-up, but Dee isn't listening any more. Gobi comes over. He has three pairs of gloves – one red, one blue, one green.

'I thought these might help,' Gobi says to Monstro. 'Red for plastic bottles, blue for cans and green for paper. This should stop it all getting mixed-up.'

Monstro goes to work again and this time his arms don't get tangled-up.

'Right, you pick up the rest,' Dee orders Mr. Scatterbrain. He starts off but the first blast of his jet-powered unicorn sets some of the rubbish on fire.

'Stop, stop,' Dee shouts, 'That's no good.' Dee and Dom whisper together. Then Dom goes to their van and comes out with a uni-cycle.

'Use this instead,' he says to Mr. Scatterbrain. 'It's much more eco-friendly.'

'But I can't ride one of those,' he protests.

'Don't worry, it'll make great TV,' Dom answers.

All the rubbish does finally get collected, but Mr. Scatterbrain is very fed-up with falling off the uni-cycle.

The next task is to clean out the pond. Nobody wants to do this as it's wet and smelly. Dom looks round and he spots Guv on his aerial soapbox.

'That's really neat,' he says. 'You can do this without getting your feet wet. Go for it Guv.'

Guv is not happy at all. He sets off slowly over the pond and tries to bend down to collect the rubbish, but his soapbox slides away and he nearly falls in.

'Brilliant, great TV!' Dee calls from the bank where she is filming.

The rest of the circus crew watch anxiously. Guv gets back safely with his rubbish bag full and his face very red and cross.

Now Dom and Dee look at the plants. 'The grass and plants need water,' Dee explains. 'Take this,' she says to Bamrod giving him a giant watering can.

Bamrod looks disappointed. 'Can't I try a different potion?' he asks.

'No,' Dee insists, 'just take this watering can and give them a good soak.'

But Bamrod thinks that just watering the grass is boring, so he waters Baked Bean as well which makes him steam like a kettle.

Dom is filming. 'Great shot,' he calls. For a moment, Bamrod thinks about watering him as well.

It's day two and time to sort out the plants. There are no Hover Bugs on Earth to make new flowers so Dom tells Tiny to plant some new seeds and young plants. But Tiny has problems at first.

'You're crushing the plants and those seeds are too deep,' Dom yells. Finally, Tiny gets the hang of it and she does a good job.

'You must have green fingers,' says Dee. Tiny looks very worried.

'Now we need to protect the seeds,' Dom says. He turns to Gobi, 'You could build a fence.'

'I could, but I won't,' Gobi mutters. 'Anyway, I've got a better idea,' and he stomps off.

Dee is talking about the broken tree. 'It won't grow again, but it will make a good home for different animals if we leave it here,' she explains to Guv. 'But we do need a new nest box for the bird that lost her nest.'

Just then Gobi appears with a fantastic scarecrow. It looks just like Guv.

'That's my second best circus suit,' Guv gasps. 'What have you done?'

But Dee is delighted and they plant the scarecrow. As they go, Guv grabs Gobi's toolbox and turns to Dom, 'This will make a good nest box, don't you think?'

'It's making good TV,' he replies.

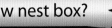

Do you think the birds will like the new nest box?

25

Only poor Baked Bean hasn't found anything useful to do. He was told off for digging up the seeds to see if they were growing. Then he got so excited that he nearly set the scarecrow on fire.

Finally Max and Lara ask him to cook some food because everyone is getting very tired and hungry as they rush to finish. Baked Bean discovers he really likes barbecues.

'I've made you something special,' he says to Dom and Dee. The burgers are a bit hotter than they expected and this time it is Lara who films them.

Finally they have done all they can. It took a long time and was hard work. The field doesn't look like it did before they arrived, but it is much better. The rubbish has all gone, the pond is clean and the new plants are starting to grow. It will take time to recover properly.

'Come back and see how it's doing in two years,' says Lara. 'We'll look after it,' promises Max.

'We'll send you a copy of the TV show – it will be great,' Dom and Dee shout.

The circus is sad to be leaving, but looking forward to a rest.

How do you think it will look in two years time?

He has forgotten all about his old toolbox.

They all agree that it was hard work, but worth it.

Can you find six things that have improved?

Look over the page for the answers.

Guv and Mrs. Spectacles keep their promise and the circus comes back in two years. They are really impressed to see how everything has changed. Max and Lara are proud of what they have done. They also have a surprise for the circus.

Dom and Dee are there too. The TV show was a great hit and they have won an award. It's a wind turbine for the circus so they can make their own electricity. Everyone is delighted, especially Gobi who will be able to look after the turbine.

Some ways to learn more about wildlife

Visit the website bbc.co.uk/breathingplaces for loads of ideas!

Keep a nature diary

- Get an exercise book – you could decorate the cover.
- When you are in the garden or on a walk, write down the plants, birds, insects and animals that you see and what they do.
- Make a note of the date and the weather as it makes it more interesting when you read it again.
- If you see something you can't identify, write down its size and colour so you can look it up in a book or online (at home or in the library) and find out what it is.

Make a bird feeder

- Punch a hole on either side of an empty plastic bottle towards the bottom.
- Push a twig all the way through with an end sticking out on both sides for perches.
- Poke more holes above the perches so birds can peck the seeds out.
- Fill the bottle with sunflower seeds or mixed seeds.
- Tie a string around the neck of the bottle and hang it from a tree.
- Ask a grown-up for help if you need to.

Did you spot?
- Plants and flowers are growing
- Butterflies and insects are back
- Frog in the pond
- Bird feeders to attract birds
- Birds are nesting
- Rubbish bins to keep it clean in future